Liliana Loretta LaRue

ANNE KELLY McGREEVY

illustrated by Fache Desrochers

NEW YORK

Liliana Loretta LaRue

Published in New York, New York, by Morgan James Publishing. Morgan James and The Entrepreneurial Publisher are trademarks of Morgan James, LLC. www.MorganJamesPublishing.com

The Morgan James Speakers Group can bring authors to your live event. For more information or to book an event visit The Morgan James Speakers Group at www.TheMorganJamesSpeakersGroup.com.

Shelfie

A **free** eBook edition is available with the purchase of this print book.

CLEARLY PRINT YOUR NAME ABOVE IN UPPER CASE

Instructions to claim your free eBook edition:
1. Download the Shelfie app for Android or iOS
2. Write your name in **UPPER CASE** above
3. Use the Shelfie app to submit a photo
4. Download your eBook to any device

ISBN 978-1-68350-069-8 paperback
ISBN 978-1-68350-070-4 eBook
Library of Congress Control Number:
2016907155

Cover Design by:
Rachel Lopez
www.r2cdesign.com

In an effort to support local communities, raise awareness and funds, Morgan James Publishing donates a percentage of all book sales for the life of each book to

Habitat for Humanity Peninsula and Greater Williamsburg.

Get involved today! Visit
www.MorganJamesBuilds.com

To the real Liliana who would never lose
anything, especially not her shoe.

Liliana Loretta LaRue

Was continually
losing her shoe.

Wherever she went

She wasn't content

Till she parted with
one of the two!

On Sunday her shoe
was brand new

When she lost it
down under the pew.

They looked high and low.

Where did that shoe go?

Not a soul in the
Church had a clue!

On Monday her shoe
was bright blue

When she left it
somewhere at the zoo.

Did the elephant see?

Oh where could it be?

Was it in with the kangaroo?

On Tuesday her
shoe really flew.

There was nothing
her mother could do.

With a huff and a puff

The wind was enough

To pull off her
shoe when it blew!

On Wednesday they
went to renew

A book that was long overdue.

She was losing herself

In the picture book shelf

When she also lost
track of her shoe.

On Thursday
that little girl knew

That the lace on
her shoe was askew

When she walked in the door

Of the big grocery store

And it dropped near
the cans of beef stew.

On Friday Miss Lily LaRue

Was wearing her favorite shoe.

On the swing or the slide

Or the carousel ride

It got lost. Where it fell,
no one knew.

On Saturday Lil took the view,

There'd be trouble
because of her shoe.

With a plop her shoe dropped

On top of a cop

And the uproar
caused quite a snafu.

Liliana Loretta LaRue

Is lamenting the loss of her shoe.

A lost ruby high-heel

Would be a big deal.

That's a shoe she'd pursue!
Wouldn't you?

Liliana Loretta LaRue

Is all finished with
losing her shoe.

Where ever she goes

She'll be showing her toes.

Going barefoot is
what she will do!

A free eBook edition is available with the purchase of this book.

To claim your free eBook edition:

1. Download the Shelfie app.
2. Write your name in uppser case in the box.
3. Use the Shelfie app to submit a photo.
4. Download your eBook to any device.

Shelfie

A **free** eBook edition is available
with the purchase of this print book.

CLEARLY PRINT YOUR NAME ABOVE IN UPPER CASE

Instructions to claim your free eBook edition:
1. Download the Shelfie app for Android or iOS
2. Write your name in **UPPER CASE** above
3. Use the Shelfie app to submit a photo
4. Download your eBook to any device

Print & Digital Together Forever.

Snap a photo

Free eBook

Read anywhere